"Witches?" Cool Beans said, in his slow-as-syrup voice. "Oh yeah, daddy-o, I'm hip to those heavy hexers."

"Can they really cast curses?" asked Natalie.

Cool Beans nodded. "Those weird sisters can blow some mighty dark juju."

"Well, we've got witches at Emerson Hicky," said Natalie.

"Do tell," Cool Beans said.

I leaned on a shelf. "And they might be casting a spell to make kids act like brats and bullies."

The big marsupial grinned. "You mean y'all need a spell to act that way?"

I rolled my eyes. "Everyone's a comedian," I said. "Seriously, could witches do that?"

The big possum stared off into space.

"Cool Beans?" said Natalie.

His voice seemed to come from the bottom of a barrel, somewhere in the next county. "Could they? Jackson, you don't *ever* wanna get in the way of a weird sister with a mad-on."

The skin on the back of my neck prickled.

"Why not?" I asked.

The librarian's shades seemed as full of darkness as Darth Vader's closet. "They might take you for a walk on the wild side," he rumbled. "And Sherlock, you might never come back."

Chet Gecko Mysteries

The Chameleon Wore Chartreuse
The Mystery of Mr. Nice
Farewell, My Lunchbag
The Big Nap
The Hamster of the Baskervilles
This Gum for Hire
The Malted Falcon
Trouble Is My Beeswax
Give My Regrets to Broadway
Murder, My Tweet
The Possum Always Rings Twice
Key Lardo
Hiss Me Deadly
From Russia with Lunch
Dial M for Mongoose

And don't miss

Chet Gecko's Detective Handbook (and Cookbook):
Tips for Private Eyes and Snack Food Lovers

From Russia with Lunch

FROM THE TATTERED CASEBOOK OF

CHET GECKO
PRIVATE EYE

Bruce Hale

sandpiper

HOUGHTON MIFFLIN HARCOURT
Boston • New York

SANDPIPER and the SANDPIPER logo are trademarks of
Houghton Mifflin Harcourt Publishing Company.

For information about permission to reproduce selections from this book,
write to trade.permissions @ hmhco.com or to Permissions, Houghton Mifflin
Harcourt Publishing Company, 3 Park Avenue, 19th Floor, New York, New York
10016

www.hmhbooks.com

The text of this book is set in Bembo.
Display type is set in Elroy.

The Library of Congress has cataloged the hardcover edition as follows:
Hale, Bruce.
From Russia with lunch/Bruce Hale.
p. cm.
Summary: Detectives Chet Gecko and his partner Natalie Attired
try to solve the mystery of why Emerson Hicky Elementary
school students have suddenly started acting strangely.
[1. Geckos—Fiction. 2. Animals—Fiction. 3. Schools—Fiction.
4. Inventions—Fiction. 5. Mystery and detective stories.
6. Humorous stories.] I. Title.
PZ7.H1295Fr 2008
[Fic]—dc22   2008004261

ISBN 978-0-15-205488-5
ISBN 978-0-547-32882-9 pb

Printed in the United States of America
DOC 10
4500767310

To Andrea with mucho aloha

A private message from the private eye . . .

I never could resist a mystery. Any mystery. Like, if Number 2 pencils are the most popular, why are they still Number 2? If a pig loses its voice, is it disgruntled? And if bedbugs live in beds and tree frogs live in trees, shouldn't box turtles come in boxes?

Of course, mysteries are meat and potatoes for a private eye. That's me, Chet Gecko, Emerson Hicky Elementary's top lizard detective. (To those who say I'm the school's *only* lizard detective, I say, "So? I'm still the *top*.")

Whenever a mystery lands on my plate, I dig right in, like a hungry worm munching a dirt sandwich. But this one time, I nearly choked on my clues.

The investigation began simply enough, with a teacher's pet acting wacko. But then the supernatural and the high tech collided, and my case took a turn for the weird.

To say I landed in a tight spot is like calling the Ice Age a wee bit of cool weather. I found myself fighting for my life with my back to the wall.

How did I win in the end? Well, as Pa Gecko always told me, there are two rules for success: 1) Don't tell all you know.

And if you want to know 2), you'll have to read the story . . .

1

All Booked Up

I didn't see it coming—not in the library.

Library period is a cheery mountain hut on the long barefoot slog up Mount Everest that is a typical school day. You expect rest and recovery. You expect books and computers, maybe a little Dewey decimalizing.

But you don't expect mayhem and mystery.

This particular library period, I was sitting on the matted green carpet with the rest of Mr. Ratnose's fourth-grade class. We were waiting for Principal Zero to get to the point.

"... And because of our school's budget *yada yada* and fiscal *blah blah blah*," the big cat rumbled, "we've decided to take strong *haminah-jaminah*."

Principal Zero was a tough but fair administrator with a massive gut and the sweet disposition of Ivan the Terrible with a toothache.

But man, that kitty could gab.

My attention wandered like a preschooler in a toy store. I eyeballed the draped shape beside the principal, as big as two refrigerators. (The shape, that is, not the principal.)

Bo Newt leaned close and muttered, "Whaddaya think that is? A new soda machine?"

"In the library?" I said. "Dream on, pal."

"Shhh!" hissed Bitty Chu, teacher's pet.

Mr. Zero tossed a glare my way, but he didn't stop flapping his gums. "And so to help with our cost cutting, we've hired an inventor."

An inventor? My ears perked up. (Or they would have, if my ears hadn't been just two holes in my head.) *Inventor* brought to mind Ben Franklin, Dr. Frankenstein, and other great men of science.

I sat up straighter.

"So let me introduce"—the burly tomcat paused dramatically—"Dr. Tanya Lightov." He clapped his paws together, leading the applause.

A woodchuck in a white lab coat stepped out from behind the mysterious thingamabob. She was as stiff as a grasshopper Popsicle. Her furry cheeks were full and sleek, and her blue eyes were colder than a Siberian snowball.

"A *girl* inventor?" I blurted.

"Da," said Dr. Lightov.

Shirley Chameleon poked me in the back. "Girls can do anything boys can, but better."

"If you're talking about spreading cooties at light-speed," I said, "you're right."

This earned me another, harder poke.

"Settle down," Mr. Zero growled. "Your class will be the first to see this new invention because Dr. Lightov is the aunt of your classmate Pete Moss."

Every eye turned to Pete, who frowned and studied his toenails. If he weren't completely covered by hair, he would've blushed redder than a cherry kissing a tomato.

Here's all you need to know about Pete Moss: If you take the world's most average student and multiply by twelve—that's Pete. He'd been in my class all year, and I barely knew the guy.

"Peter, dahling," said Dr. Lightov, "vould you kindly help me?"

The little brown groundhog shrugged. He looked like he'd rather perform dental surgery on a grizzly bear, but he rose and shuffled forward.

His aunt told us, "Zhis machine vill automate all ze vork in ze library. Storytime, book selection, checkout—everyzhing."

Bitty Chu's hand shot up. "But what about our librarian, Cool Beans?" she asked. "What will he do?"

Principal Zero cleared his throat. "He will be, ah, leaving us."

"*Leaving?*" I said. "No way!"

I turned to the huge possum leaning up against a bookshelf. He offered a sleepy smile. "Cool your jets, Jackson," said the librarian.

"But what'll you do?" I asked.

"I'll make the scene back in the bayou. Either banging the bongos in a jazz band or vampire hunting. Haven't decided yet."

No more Cool Beans?

My jaw clenched. However nifty this invention might be, it wasn't worth losing one of the school's few decent teachers.

But before I could protest, Dr. Lightov whipped the sheet off her invention. "Behold," she said, "ze amazing Bibliomalgamator!"

"Ooh!" went my classmates.

The gleaming silver contraption sported a bank of lights and switches and monitors. The doctor pressed a red button. Everything lit up and whirred.

I hated to admit it, but it *was* pretty slick.

"Ve insert ze books through zhis port," the woodchuck said. She and Pete lugged armloads of novels from a nearby shelf and slipped them one by one into a wide hole.

"Zhen ve program ze readers' choices on zhis

keyboard," said Dr. Lightov. As Pete kept adding books, she asked several kids what they liked to read.

"Mysteries," said Waldo the furball.

"Romance," said Shirley. I shuddered.

Jackdaw Ripper belched. "Anything with blood and guts in it," he said.

The inventor's fingers danced over the keyboard. She hit a blue button, and the machine went *beep-boop-bop!*

"And now," she said. "Ze Bibliomalgamator vill provide your recommended reading."

My three classmates stood and approached the gizmo. Dr. Lightov twisted a dial and turned to us with a chilly smile.

"So you see," she said, "my invention is much more efficient zhen ze old-fashioned librarian."

The book machine rumbled and whined. *Thoomp*—a book slid down a chute into Jackdaw's grasp.

"*Tales of Miss Smoochy-Pants*?" he said. "Where's the blood and guts in that?"

Dr. Lightov looked like she'd swallowed a stapler. She coughed and turned another knob. "Zhere," she said. "Now you vill see . . ."

With a loud buzz, the contraption began to shake. Then, *whap-bap-whomp!* It spat out book after book.

The first few plowed into Jackdaw, knocking him flat.

"It's *alive!*" cried Waldo. He turned to run, and the machine rifled a dictionary into his back, slamming him into the shelves.

"*Yaah!*" cried my classmates. We scrambled aside as books flew through the air.

Mr. Zero caught a stack of Hardly Boys Mysteries in his padded gut. "Do something!" he snarled at Dr. Lightov.

She and Pete fluttered about, punching buttons and twisting dials. But the book machine gun kept firing.

Finally, Cool Beans ambled over and yanked the plug from the wall.

Wheeeeeoooooh, sighed the book machine. With one last *ptoo,* it spat a copy of *Hairy Plotter IV* onto Jackdaw's chest.

"Well," said the librarian. "Looks like I won't be packin' my bags as soon as all that."

2

Little Bitty, Gritty One

After all the ruckus in the library, I needed something to fortify my inner gecko. While many of my classmates went to check out Dr. Lightov's new lunch-dispensing Munchmeister 2000, I grabbed my sack lunch and made for the scrofulous tree.

I was glad to be brown bagging. I like to eat my lunch, not wear it.

Ma Gecko's peanut butter-pickle-and-mayfly sandwich hit the spot. Since my partner, Natalie Attired, was off helping her teacher, I crunched my doodlebug lemon crisps in silence.

Silence felt weird. Detectives don't like peace and quiet.

Strolling back to my room after the class bell rang,

I felt antsy. I wished for a case. I wished for a mystery. I wished for a little excitement.

Oh, silly gecko.

I got much more than I bargained for.

Mr. Ratnose's classroom was unusually rowdy that day. Kids chattered and argued and laughed. Bitty Chu, the gopher, swaggered down the aisle to her seat and slammed into my shoulder as she passed.

"Easy there, Poindexter!" I said. "First day with the new legs?"

She just curled her lip and sauntered on. Odd. But then, I've never understood those teacher's pets. (Anyone who'd rather study than watch cartoons is a mystery to me.)

Mr. Ratnose tried to get us to focus.

"Settle down, class!" he said.

Most of the kids took their seats. But Bitty, Jack-daw Ripper, and the boring field mouse Olive Drabb kept standing, yakking away.

Our teacher cleared his throat. "People, sit down! Now!"

Bitty swiveled her head and fixed her favorite teacher with the kind of stare that bullies usually turn on me. "Make me, Teach," she grunted.

I sat up. *This* was interesting.

Mr. Ratnose's eyes bugged out like a bullfrog's throat on a hot June night. "Wh-what did you say?"

"Why should I listen to you? You're full of mean-ingless blather." Even with her tough new talk, Bitty still had a teacher's pet's vocabulary.

"That's right," chorused Olive and Jackdaw Ripper. "Meaningless blabber."

I glanced at them. The class punk and the class drudge agreeing with the teacher's pet?

Something was out of whack.

Mr. Ratnose looked like he'd just discovered a live scorpion in his coffee. But he bounced back. "Miss Chu, Mr. Ripper, and Miss Drabb," snapped the lean rat, "if you don't sit down and be quiet, I'm sending you to the principal's office."

"Ooh, I'm shakin'," Jackdaw said.

"Shakin' like bacon," droned Olive.

Mr. Ratnose's eyes burned like Cajun-fried cockroaches. "I have never heard such impertinence," he said.

"Then you need to clean out your earwax," Bitty sneered, hands on hips.

My teacher's whiskers bristled. His voice grew flatter than a spider under a rolling pin.

"You all just earned a trip to Mr. Zero's office," he said. "Move it!"

The rat grabbed Bitty's paw and Jackdaw's wing. Herding Olive before them, he made for the door.

"Silent reading, everyone," said Mr. Ratnose over

his shoulder. "I'll be back in a few minutes." He glared. "And don't anyone else get any ideas."

I swiveled in my chair to watch them go.

Curiouser and curiouser. What was going on?

Apparently someone else was wondering the same thing. When I turned to face the front, Igor Beaver was standing by my desk.

"Um, hi," he said.

"Hi, yourself, bright boy."

Of our three teacher's pets—Igor, Cassandra, and Bitty—Igor was the teacher's pettiest. His short-sleeved white shirt was held closed by a dorky bow tie, just like the one Mr. Ratnose wore. His buck-toothed mouth was as likely to tattle on a classmate as to gnaw a Number 2 pencil.

Igor Beaver put the *gee* in geek. So what did he want with me?

I asked him.

"It's about Bitty," he said.

"Your psycho pal?"

"She's, um, not herself today," said Igor.

I pushed my hat back. "Who is she, Bertha Back-talk?"

His beady eyes grew shiny. "I'm worried about her. Bitty was fine before lunch, then she just, um, flipped out. She wouldn't even do flash cards with me."

I glanced at the rest of my classmates, who were yakking away. "Okay," I said. "So, what do you want me to do about it?"

"You're an investigator," said Igor. "Can't you, um, investigate?" He plucked a yellow pencil from his pocket and began nibbling on it.

A client? An actual case? My tail curled.

I covered my excitement with a yawn. It never hurts to play hard to get. "You want me to find out what's wrong with your little pal? It'll cost you."

Igor dug in his pocket and pulled out two quarters, a massive wad of lint, an Albert Einstein trading card, and a calculator. He forked over the coins.

"Will fifty cents do?"

I jingled the cool quarters in my palm. "I like the sound of your money," I said. "But not your story. What's your angle, pal?"

Igor's eyes shifted. "I don't know what you mean."

"Come on, egghead. You're not doing this because you're full of the milk of rodent kindness. So Bitty bugged out. What's it to you?"

Igor gnawed his pencil. "She and I are on the math team. And we can't beat Petsadena Elementary if Bitty's thrown off the squad for, um, misbehaving."

I cocked my head. "Fair enough, Bucky. You just bought yourself a detective. Now, tell the nice PI all about it."

3

Stu Pigeon

Late recess found me nosing around the school yard in search of two things: my partner and a snack. I hit the candy machine first. (A detective has his priorities.)

Munching from a bag of Skeeter Pieces, I went after the second thing. As I passed the basketball courts, a whip-smart mockingbird was perched on a low wall, holding court to a handful of kids.

"Here's another one," she said, eyes twinkling. "A guy walks into a doctor's office with a cucumber up his nose, a carrot in his left ear, and a banana in his right ear. He says, 'What's the matter with me?' And the doctor says—"

"You're not eating properly," I interrupted.

The kids chuckled. The mockingbird turned to look.

"And here I thought you didn't like my jokes," said Natalie Attired.

I smirked. "Just the bad ones. Got time for a case, partner?"

"As long as it's not a case of chicken pox." Natalie bowed and waved to her audience. "Thanks, you've been great. See you next recess. Don't forget to tip your lunch lady."

Puzzled but smiling, the kids wandered off.

"What's the buzz, cuz?" said Natalie. "Blackmail, kidnapping, vampires on the loose?"

"I wish," I said. "A teacher's pet wigged out."

Natalie arched an eyebrow. "Not much of a case. And for that you interrupted my routine?"

I shrugged. "Not much of a routine. Let's head out."

The quickest way to the bottom of this investigation was to get the hot scoop straight from the gopher's mouth. We'd talk Bitty into spilling the beans, solve her problem, and collect some more coins from Igor.

What could be easier?

Bitty Chu was slumped on a bench near the gym. She looked lower than a snake's belt buckle.

"Cheer up, sister," I said. "Help is here."

The gopher regarded us with dull eyes. "Oh, you."

She seemed nothing like the rude rodent who had stirred up all that trouble in class.

"Something bothering you?" said Natalie.

"Me?" said Bitty. "I sassed my favorite teacher and got kicked off the math team. What could possibly be bothering me?"

I cleared my throat. "Easy there. Sarcasm is *my* department. Just tell us why you flipped out."

"It might make you feel better," said Natalie.

The gopher's gaze went from one of us to the other. She looked bluer than tarantula tootsies in the Arctic Ocean.

"It might," said Bitty, tearing up. "If I *knew* why. But I . . . *sniff* . . . don't . . . *sniff* . . . know why-*hy-hy*!" She sobbed into her paws.

I hate it when dames turn on the waterworks. (*Dames,* in case you don't know, is what we private eyes call girls.)

"Something must have set you off," I said.

"Nothing," Bitty whimpered.

"Problems at home?" asked Natalie.

Bitty shook her head.

"Problems with Mr. Ratnose?" I asked.

"No," she sobbed.

I twirled my finger beside my head. "Lost your marbles?"

"No!"

Natalie rested a wing tip on the gopher's shoulder. "Is it . . . boy trouble?"

"I don't have a boyfriend to have trouble with." Bitty sniffed.

Natalie nodded. "Maybe *that's* your trouble."

I held up my hands. "Hang on. Are you telling me you have no idea why you mouthed off to Mr. Ratnose?"

The gopher peered up at me through her paws. "That's *exactly* what I've been telling you."

"Oh." I looked at Natalie. She looked at me. We were fresh out of ideas.

"It was like I was in this haze," said Bitty. "Words came out of my mouth, but I couldn't stop them— almost like I was under a spell."

"A spell?" I repeated. "Like a witch spell?"

"How do *I* know which spell?" said Bitty.

I shook my head. "No, not *which*, witch."

The gopher clenched her fists. "I just told you I don't *know* which."

"I think he meant—" said Natalie.

Bitty stood. "Enough!" she snapped, and stomped off.

"You sure do have a way with girls," said Natalie.

I stuck a hand in my pocket. "Hey, at least she stopped crying."

"So what now, Mr. PI? We search for ladies on brooms with pointy hats?"

Pulling out the rest of my Skeeter Pieces, I said, "Not exactly. I think I know where to get the lowdown on witches. And all it takes is a little chocolate."

Hustling to beat the clock, we hotfooted it for Stu Pigeon's perch. With a little luck and pluck, we might learn something before recess ended.

Stu Pigeon was the school yard snitch. He liked to hang out on a twisted krangleberry bush at the playground's edge, the better to watch the action.

His gray-feathered head bobbed and weaved like a punch-drunk fighter. His stubby beak was built for sniffing out scandal. And his shifty eyes could count your lunch money to the penny from a half mile away on a foggy morning.

Rumor and gossip were Stu's bread and butter. When he saw us coming, he flinched.

"I didn't do it," he said.

"Do what?" I asked.

"Whatever it was you think I did," said Stu. He opened his wings to take off.

I held up a hand. "Whoa there, Nervous Nick. We're here on business."

Stu eyed us warily. "*Trouble* is your business. I don't like trouble."

"I thought trouble *kept* you in business," said Natalie.

The pigeon looked from me to her. Then he settled back down. "You got me there. So what's up? Buying or selling information?"

"Buying." I shook the partial bag of Skeeter Pieces.

"Eh," said Stu. "You ain't buying much."

I held the bag up where he could see it. "We're investigating a certain teacher's pet who jumped the rails."

Stu squinted. "Skipped school?"

"Sassed a teacher," said Natalie. "She said she couldn't help herself, like she was under a spell."

I leaned closer. "Heard of any spell-casting types around school? You know, witches, warlocks, funky zombie masters?"

Stu's head bobbed. He checked left, then right. "Wouldn't have to be a spell," he said. "You could do the same thing with chemicals."

"What chemicals?" asked Natalie.

He shrugged. "Beats me. What do I look like, Elmo Einstein?"

"Did you hear someone discussing—?" said Natalie.

I cut her off. "Never mind the chemicals. Tell us about the spell-casters."

For a second, Natalie looked hurt. "The chemicals are a good lead."

"Maybe, but I have a hunch about the voodoo," I said. "Come on, Stu."

With a last glance over his shoulder, Stu spilled the beans. "I got something."

"Yeah?" I said.

He stared pointedly at my candy.

"Oh, yeah." I tossed him the bag, and Stu scarfed it up.

"*Mmm,* sweet Skeeters," he said. "All right, look, there's this bunch of kids that meets at lunch, over by the yew."

"The *me*?" I said.

Natalie rolled her eyes. "It's a kind of tree, Chet. But I guess that's a new one on yew."

I groaned. "Oak-kay," I said. "Enough funny stuff. So these kids meet at lunch by some goofy tree. And . . . ?"

Stu made with the bobbing and weaving again. Satisfied that nobody could overhear, he said, "Rumor has it that these girls are witches."

I smiled. "Now we're getting somewhere. What are their names?"

The pigeon poked at the empty candy wrapper. "Names?" he scoffed. "You want names, bring more candy."

"Never mind," I said. "We'll use our private-eye skills to get the names."

Just then the class bell rang: *B-r-r-r-ring!*

Stu jumped. "And what do your PI skills tell you about that?"

"That if we don't get our tails back to class now, we'll be in trouble."

Stu shook his head mockingly. "And they said you couldn't be taught."

4

Witch and Famous

There was no point in searching for witches until the next lunchtime, so I hunkered down for the rest of Mr. Ratnose's lessons. Ah, the simple joys of schoolwork. It was no more excruciating than being dipped in stinkbug oil and roasted over hot coals.

It just felt that way.

The classroom rebellion seemed to have died down. Nobody sassed the teacher all afternoon. Not even me.

The school day ended, as school days must. Evening came, bringing homework, dinner, and bratty little sisters—not in any particular order.

The next morning I was champing at the bit. I couldn't wait for lunchtime. (Of course, most days are like that.)

My mom had packed me a sack lunch again. Still, I cruised through the cafeteria at lunchtime to eyeball Dr. Lightov's Munchmeister 2000.

It squatted behind the counter, as massive as the front four on a refrigerator football team. Colored lights played over its dark surface like rainbows in a root beer. Kids punched one of three buttons: Burrito Maximus, County Fair Dogs, or Spicy Pizza.

A little vole chose the pizza option. The machine clicked and whirred. A bowl dropped into place, and a stream of grayish gloop poured from a spout. Half sprayed on the vole, half ended up in her bowl.

She cocked her head. "*That's* pizza?"

My thoughts exactly.

"Hi, Chet," came a totally average voice.

I glanced around, looking for its source. Finally I spotted him right by the machine. "Oh, Pete," I said. "I didn't notice you."

Pete Moss pouted. "The story of my life."

Dr. Tanya Lightov stepped from behind her contraption. "Ve have created ze perfect puree—nutritionally balanced and delicious. Enjoy!" She wiped the gloop from the vole with a dirty rag and handed her the bowl.

"But—" said the little rodent.

"I said, *Enjoy!*"

The vole took her food and shuffled off.

"Zhese children," muttered the inventor. "Sometimes I could just—" She noticed me watching her. "Vell? If you don't vant my lunch, move along!"

I moved.

Natalie was already waiting at our informal office, the scrofulous tree by the edge of the playground. She broke out her wormy apple crisp (with extra worms), while I tucked into leftover mothloaf in aphid sauce.

For a few minutes, there was nothing but munching. At last, I stood, crumpled my brown bag, and chucked it into a nearby trash can.

"Ready to grill some witches?" I asked.

Natalie slurped one last worm. "Chet, you don't really believe in witches, do you?"

"Not really." I stepped out onto the grass. "But I didn't believe in zombie masters or ghosts, either."

"And we've already faced both of those."

I nodded. "Exactly. This is one screwy school, partner."

As we ankled on over to the yew tree, I scanned the playground. Aside from the normal ball games, two girls were chasing a boy, three second graders were stuffing a sixth-grade badger into a trash can, and several fluffy bunnies had treed a lynx.

I shook my head in amusement. The usual lunchtime hijinks.

"Looks like everyone's stirred up," said Natalie.

"Naw, just a little spring fever."

"In January?"

I shrugged. "Kids will be kids."

Natalie frowned. "I swear, Chet, it really stinks when you just ignore my opinions like tha—"

Suddenly a voice cried, "Look out!"

I whipped around to see a huge, tractorlike rig bearing down on us. Natalie and I hopped aside. It rumbled past.

Maureen DeBree, the school's mongoose custodian, rode atop the beast. She waved an apology. "Still learning how for steer," she called, mowing down two small bushes.

Ms. DeBree veered back onto the grass. The tractor-thingie seemed to be a combination lawn mower, leaf sweeper, and hedge trimmer.

Blades and rakes sprouted from its sides like the legs of a robot tarantula. A vacuum on the back sucked leaves and grass trimmings into its maw. Curly silver letters on its side spelled out THE YARD CZAR.

"A new laborsaving invention?" I shouted.

"Yeah," cried the mongoose. "Like they say, a stick in time saves nine!"

And in a belch of blue smoke, she trundled off.

"Dr. Lightov's been busy," said Natalie.

"Busier than a one-armed trombone player in a marching band," I said.

Natalie smoothed her feathers. We pressed onward.

Just ahead, seven girls sat in a circle of white stones beneath an evergreen tree. As we approached, they were chanting with eyes closed. Sweet smoke drifted from a smoldering stick in the middle.

"Maybe I should handle this," Natalie muttered.

"Nonsense," I said. "Dames can't resist my charm."

We stopped at the edge of the circle. Now I could make out their chant:

> "Sisters seven, strong are we;
>   By the power of stone and tree;
>   Far from city steel and noise;
>   Far from rude and smelly boys—"

I cleared my throat. "Nice tune. Now how about the dance-mix version?"

Seven sets of eyes blinked open. The girls looked as friendly and welcoming as a school of piranhas sizing up a fat, juicy transfer student.

"And who might you be?" asked a tall alligator lizard in a purple, flowered T-shirt.

"I might be a yellow-bellied sapsucker," I said. "But they call me Chet Gecko. This is my partner, Natalie."

A green-spotted toad blinked at me. "You don't belong here."

"True," I said. "But unless Principal Zero gives me time off for good behavior, here I'll be through sixth grade."

Purple Tee narrowed her eyes. "Run along, little gecko."

"No can do, Stretch," I said. "We're on a case."

Natalie pushed forward. "A girl in Chet's class went a little crazy yesterday; she couldn't help herself. We were wondering—"

"Did you put a spell on her?" I said.

A tabby kitten blinked her big blue eyes. "A spell?"

"Yeah, you know—a jinx, a curse, a whammy?"

"Us?" said the kitty.

"Don't play innocent, pussycat," I said. "You're witches, right? And witches cast spells."

Purple Tee stood. "We're *Wicca*."

"I don't care how wicked you are," I said. "If you hexed my classmate, I'm bringing you down."

"That's Wic-*ca*," said Spotty, joining Purple Tee. "We're peaceful, nature-worshipping—"

"Witches," I said. "Fess up—did you put the evil eye on Bitty Chu?"

"Evil eye?!" Spotty spluttered.

Three more of the crew stood up. For a bunch

of peace-loving nature girls, they looked as full of trouble as a werewolf's smile.

Natalie put her wing tip on my arm. "Perhaps we could talk another time."

I sized up the situation. Nobody was rushing to confess. Heck, nobody even wanted to talk with us. I tipped my hat. "Ladies."

As Natalie and I rambled off, seven pairs of eyes drilled a hole in my back.

"Let *you* handle everything?" said Natalie.

"What?" I said. "I charmed them."

"Into hating us."

I turned my palms up. "What can I say? I've got the magic touch."

5

Year of the Brat

The last dribbles of lunch period were leaking out, like the sauce from a Sloppy Junebug sandwich. Natalie and I paused on the grassy slope of the playground to regroup.

"Maybe we're looking at this all wrong," she said.

"All right, I'll try squinting."

Natalie smirked. "That reminds me—when your nose runs and your feet smell, what are you?"

I could feel the joke coming, but I couldn't stop it.

"Upside down!" she cackled.

I sighed. "Okay, okay, back to your brainstorm."

Natalie preened her wing feathers. "Didn't you once tell me not to guess whodunit before all the facts are in?"

"Yeah . . ."

"So let's check the facts, Jack." We wandered toward the basketball courts.

"Okay . . . ," I said. "Fact: Bitty Chu did a really fine impression of a punk yesterday, along with Olive Drabb and Jackdaw, who really *is* a punk."

"Fact: Bitty flipped out right after lunch period, but by late recess she was back to normal," Natalie said.

I grinned. "Or what passes for normal with a teacher's pet."

Natalie stooped and picked up a basketball. "So don't you see?"

"What?"

"Maybe what happened to Bitty happened to Olive, too." She passed me the ball. "And maybe their freaky behavior had something to do with what took place at lunch."

I dribbled and took a shot. "What took place at lunch?"

Pang! The ball banged off the rim. Natalie chased it.

"Search me," she said. "What goes on at lunchtime?"

"Um, eating," I said.

"Playing," said Natalie, dribbling the ball.

"Hexing. And, uh . . ." I halfheartedly tried to block her.

Natalie flapped one wing for altitude and shot with the other.

Swishh! Basket.

"So maybe they ate some bad doodlebug casserole," she said.

I retrieved the ball and dribbled some more. "You're saying Bitty went loco from some funky food, not from a witch's spell?"

She raised her eyebrows. "It's worth checking out."

"That could be," I said as the class bell rang. "But I know one thing for sure."

"What's that?" asked Natalie.

"We'll have to check it out at recess. Mr. Ratnose gets prickly when I investigate during class time."

I expected the next two lessons to be about as lively as an all-day tour of the Used Gum Museum. But, as sometimes happens, I was wrong.

Mr. Ratnose could barely say two sentences without being interrupted. Bitty was in fine bratty form again. And she was joined by about half of the class, including my client, Igor Beaver.

So many smart-aleck remarks flew through the air that I started taking notes. Ten kids were sent to the principal's office. Four more had to write *I will not sass the teacher* on the blackboard. And the rest of us were forced to do silent reading while Mr. Ratnose silently tore out his whiskers.

It was a strange day, no doubt.

I thought about what Natalie had said. Maybe she was right. Maybe the food, the witches, or something had put the whammy on all those kids at lunchtime, not just Bitty.

But how to learn what these troublemakers had in common? Hmm. If I could just find a bunch of them gathered together . . .

A smile stretched my lips. I raised my hand.

"Oh, Mr. Ratnose?"

He looked up from his papers. One eye was twitching. "Yes, Chester Gecko?"

I hate when they call me by my full name.

"Can I go to the principal's office?" I asked.

The slim rat frowned. "It's *may I*," he said, "and no, you may not."

"Please?" I said.

"No."

"Pleeease?"

"*No.* Get back to your reading."

I waited a couple of seconds for his nerves to stretch to the breaking point. "Pretty please, with sugared sweat bees on top?"

Mr. Ratnose erupted from his seat. "*No!* NO! A thousand times no!" Chest heaving, he scribbled on his pink pad, tore off a sheet and thrust it at me. "Go straight to the principal's office, and stay there until you learn some manners!"

I smirked as I collected the slip. Who says being polite never gets you anywhere?

I could hear the hubbub from down the hall. The administration building sounded like a summer camp cabin hopped up on s'mores and sleeplessness.

Pushing open the door, I surveyed the scene.

About fifty kids packed the waiting area, jabbering, arguing, flinging paper clips, and generally causing a ruckus. I spotted model students and bullies alike, all behaving like junior thugs.

Bitty Chu was yelling at a parrot. Igor Beaver was thwacking a squirrel with a rubber band.

I fought my way to Igor's side. "We're making progress on the case."

"Big whoop," he snarled.

"Don't you care about the math team?" I said.

He aimed the rubber band at me. "Math, schmath."

"We'll talk later," I said, and slipped away.

Mrs. Crow, the school secretary, had retreated behind her counter. Her feathers were ruffled, her eyes wild.

"Settle down, you monsters!" she croaked.

I noticed Principal Zero's door was ajar. How in the world could he ignore all this noise? Edging past a pair of battling bluebirds, I moved along the wall and poked my head into his office.

The big cat was head-to-head with Dr. Tanya Lightov.

"If you ask me," she was saying, "ve could solve zhis in no time."

"How's that?" said Mr. Zero.

"A simple chip implant, and all ze behavior problems vanish."

The principal scowled. "Turning students into robots is *not* the answer. We—" Just then, he noticed me snooping. "Gecko, shut that door!"

"Aye, aye, boss man," I said. I left them to their chat and got back to my investigation.

Talking sense to this mob wouldn't be easy. I stuck my little fingers in my mouth and gave a piercing whistle.

The racket lowered a notch or two. Heads turned.

"Greetings, sports fans," I said. "A couple of questions."

"Stuff a sock in it, Gecko!" cried the parrot.

"Yeah!" several nerds-turned-punks shouted.

I hopped up onto the counter. "Have any of you ticked off the witches?"

"Witches?" said a burly badger. "Which witches?"

"Stuff a shoe in it, Gecko!" cried the parrot.

The noise level rose. Students started shoving one another again. I only had a few seconds more before I lost them.

"How many of you ate lunch in the cafeteria today?" I shouted.

A few kids raised their hands. Most just glared or ignored me.

"The pizza tasted like glue," the badger growled.

"Stuff some, uh, glue in it, Gecko!" said the parrot.

A skunk snarled, "Who said you could ask us questions, anyway?"

"Yeah!" the crowd yelled.

"I'm Chet Gecko, Private Eye. Questions come with the job."

The skunk bared her teeth. "Well, I think you're a nosy nitwit."

I bristled. "And I think you're a stink bomb with stripes."

"Get him!" cried the badger. They surged for me. Then the skunk turned and did a handstand.

How nice, I thought, *she's a gymnast.*

But then the little voice in my head said, *She's no gymnast. That's what they do just before they spray.*

My legs turned to lead. I was caught dead in the crosshairs.

Maybe you shouldn't have made that crack about the stink bomb, said the little voice.

"Now you tell me," I muttered.

6

By Hook or By Cookie

"*Aaah!*" The troublemakers scattered like cockroaches under a spotlight.

I leaped from the counter onto the side wall—just in time.

Pffffffhhht!

The skunk blasted her stench like a pirate's cannon. *Boom!* Right into Mrs. Crow.

"*Eeeuch!*" the secretary cried. "You are in *big* trouble, girlie!"

The skunk noticed that she'd missed her target. When she spotted me on the wall, the little stinker spun around for another try.

I decided not to wait and see if her aim improved. Quick as a hungry flea, I zipped along the wall and out the open doorway.

Pfffffhhht!

The second blast whizzed past, nailing Mr. Kent Hoyt, bad-tempered bobcat and sixth-grade teacher.

"Ree*oww*!" Mr. Hoyt reeled back, wiping his eyes and cursing. Then, with a savage growl, he dived through the door.

I considered for a moment: Should I go back in? The office was wall-to-wall punks. One mischief-maker more or less wouldn't make any difference.

Down the hall I went.

Something was seriously screwy at this school. It had gone beyond spring fever and heebie-jeebies into some kind of full-on flu.

And Dr. Gecko had to find the cure.

My feet turned toward the cafeteria. I was starting to think that Natalie's hunch about the lunches might be right. And even if it wasn't, at least the lunchroom was a place to start.

The dimly lit building reeked of lemon floor wax, stale milk, and peanut butter—the after-smells of a thousand meals. Someone was clattering around in the kitchen. I eased up to the gleaming steel counter.

Peering around the Munchmeister 2000, I spotted the broad back of Emerson Hicky's head cafeteria lady, Mrs. Bagoong. A burly iguana with a heart of gold (or at least chocolate), Mrs. Bagoong was my connection for second helpings in the lunch line.

She was all right. For an iguana.

But just then, the queen of the lunchroom was making a strange sniffling sound.

"Caught a cold there, Brown Eyes?" I said.

She turned. Mrs. Bagoong's mouth pulled down and her eyes were watery.

"Oh, Chet, honey," she said. "I had to do somethin' real hard this morning."

"Give mouth-to-mouth resuscitation to the aspara-gasp?"

She shook her leathery head. "No use trying to cheer me up. I had to lay off my assistant chef."

"Lay off?" I said. "Like, fire him?"

"That's right. With this new machine, we only need one cook: me. I prepare the raw materials and the Munchmeister turns them into lunch."

Hmm. This was the second staff member to get the boot, if you counted Cool Beans's close call. A fired chef, eh? Maybe this guy had been mad enough to squirt loony juice in the school lunches.

"What's his name?" I asked.

"Albert Dentay."

I'd seen the guy. A solemn bullfrog, he hopped about the lunchroom, rarely saying a word.

"Do you think old Al might have put something funny in the gloop?" I asked.

The big iguana frowned. "What do you mean?"

I told her about the recent rash of nutty behavior. "It could be witches, but it might be, well, lunches."

40

Mrs. Bagoong straightened. "My food is healthy and nutritious," she huffed.

"I know, but—"

"*You* never had a problem asking for seconds."

I held up my palms. "Whoa now, Top Chef. Nobody's knocking your chow. I'm just asking, could Al have monkeyed with the food?"

The iguana glanced over at the lunch machine, then back at me.

"Maybe," she grunted. "Things get mighty busy around here."

"So keep an eye out for him," I said.

She sniffed. "If anybody's slippin' something into the food, it's that inventor."

"Dr. Lightov?"

Mrs. Bagoong folded her thick arms. "I don't like the crisp of her bacon."

"You think she might be a few eggs short of an omelet?" I asked.

The lunchroom queen raised an eyebrow. "Why just yesterday, she was goin' on about her precious gadgets. She claims she wants to make our school efficient, but I don't think she even likes the students."

I cocked my head. "Huh. That's food for thought. And speaking of food . . ."

"Yes?"

"You don't happen to have any *real* food around here, do you?"

For the first time, a slight smile curled her lips. "Well, as a matter of fact, I like to bake when I'm feeling blue. And I just whipped up a batch of peanut butter bark-bug cookies."

My eyes went as big around as dinner plates. My stomach rumbled.

"Care to have some?" asked Mrs. Bagoong.

I licked my lips. "Sister, we'd be fools not to."

7

Knock on Woodchuck

Time sure flies when you're eating cookies. As I finished my snack break, I noticed it was almost second recess.

Leaving the cafeteria with pockets loaded, I had more than cookies to chew on. I had another suspect to investigate.

When the bell rang, I was waiting under the scrofulous tree for my partner. Soon, Natalie glided to a landing.

"Chet, you gotta hear this one," she said. "Why was Cinderella such a lousy soccer player?"

"Search me. Why?"

"Because she ran away from the ball and had a pumpkin for a coach!" Natalie cackled. "Get it?"

I got it. With Natalie, there was no missing it.

"Can you spare some time from your joke telling?" I asked.

"Depends," she said. "Is it for our case?"

I filled her in on the latest—the mob scene in the office, the disgruntled chef.

"I think the inventor's behind it," said Natalie.

I chuckled. "Dr. Lightov? I don't think so."

"Why not?"

"First off, she's a dame."

"Hey!" Natalie squawked.

"Sorry, a *lady*." I stood and started walking. "And I don't think a da—lady could pull off an underhanded caper like this."

Natalie followed. "Oh, yeah? How about Mata Hari, Nadia Nyce, and other female masterminds?"

"Okay, okay, *maybe* you've got a point," I said. "But why would Dr. Lightov sabotage her own invention?"

Natalie shrugged. "Part of her evil plan for world domination?"

I stopped and looked at her. "You won't give up on this until we eliminate her as a suspect, will you?"

"Nope."

I blew out a sigh. "Come on, let's go get the lowdown from her nephew."

"Zhis ees mahvelous idea," said Natalie, in a dead-on impression of Tanya Lightov.

After a brief search, we tracked down Pete Moss. The woodchuck was all by his lonesome at the edge of the playground.

I gave him a cheery greeting. "What do you know, Joe?"

"My name is Pete." He pouted.

"I know," I said. "But 'how're your feet, Pete' just doesn't have the same ring. You know my partner, Natalie?"

The groundhog nodded, looking down. "Yeah, you two investigate things."

Natalie smiled encouragingly. "That's right. We just wanted to ask you a few questions about your aunt."

"My aunt?" Pete's lower lip stuck out far enough to make a landing strip for a family of gooney birds.

"Is something wrong?" asked Natalie.

"No," said Pete, scuffing at

the grass with a foot. "It is just . . . embarrassing, having a famous relative."

"I know exactly how you feel," I said. "My grandpa Gecko was a trapeze artist. For a long time, he got all the attention, and I was sore."

"Then what happened?" Pete looked up.

"I got into the swing of things," I said.

Natalie groaned.

"But we didn't come here to make funny," I said. "Let's talk about your aunt."

"What about her?" Pete wandered toward the sandbox. We joined him.

"How does she feel about the school?" asked Natalie.

The groundhog lifted a shoulder. "She likes it, I guess."

"And the students?" I asked. "She likes them, too?"

Pete gave me a sideways look. "Sure, why not?"

"She doesn't have any grudges against anyone?" said Natalie.

He scowled. "Why all the questions?"

"No reason," I said. "We're nosy."

Pete stopped at the edge of the sandbox and chewed his lip. "I cannot think of anyone she holds a grudge against. Except my dad. But that is family."

He sat down and started aimlessly digging a hole. Groundhogs do that.

I caught Natalie's attention and waggled my eyebrows. "Okay then," I said. "Thanks for your help."

"Um, bye, now," said Natalie. She looked a question at me as we took off.

"Why didn't we stick with him?" she muttered.

"I know you suspect Dr. Lightov, but it's a dead end," I said. "She has no motive, and Pete was about as useful as a kickstand on a tricycle. We tried."

My footsteps led toward the library.

"So, are you planning to tell me where we're going, or do I have to get psychic?" Natalie asked.

"Should be pretty easy," I said. "You're already psycho."

"Ha, ha."

I pushed back my hat and let the sun warm my face. "All right. Since we can't check out Albert Dentay until after school, I thought we might get some background info on those witches, just to be thorough."

Natalie glanced at the library. "Are you planning to look them up on Witchi-pedia?"

"Naw," I said. "I thought we'd chat with our local expert on the supernatural."

"Cool Beans," said Natalie.

"Partner, you read my mind."

She smirked. "I've seen picture books that were harder to read."

We found the massive possum shelving books. He took a breather and sat back on his haunches.

"Witches?" Cool Beans said, in his slow-as-syrup voice. "Oh yeah, daddy-o, I'm hip to those heavy hexers."

"Can they really cast curses?" asked Natalie. "I mean, does it work?"

Cool Beans nodded. "Those weird sisters can blow some mighty dark juju."

"How do you mean?" I asked.

"One time, I saw this cat get turned into a wiener dog." The possum adjusted his blue beret. "And we're talkin' a *real* cat, not a cool cat."

"Well, we've got witches at Emerson Hicky," said Natalie.

"Do tell," Cool Beans said.

I leaned on a shelf. "And they might be casting a spell to make kids act like brats and bullies."

The big marsupial grinned. "You mean y'all need a spell to act that way?"

I rolled my eyes. "Everyone's a comedian," I said. "Seriously, could witches do that?"

"Most witches are peaceful, tree-huggin' types," said the librarian.

"Yeah, yeah. But if they wanted to, could they curse the kids?"

The big possum stared off into space.

"Cool Beans?" said Natalie.

His voice seemed to come from the bottom of a barrel, somewhere in the next county. "Could they? Jackson, you don't *ever* wanna get in the way of a weird sister with a mad-on."

The skin on the back of my neck prickled.

"Why not?" I asked.

The librarian's shades seemed as full of darkness as Darth Vader's closet. "They might take you for a walk on the wild side," he rumbled. "And Sherlock, you might never come back."

The bell rang, the mood was broken, and we returned to class. But all the way, Cool Beans's words stayed with me.

To solve this investigation, I might have to confront those witches.

And if he was right, I could be risking much more than a slap on the wrist.

Dang. I *hate* it when cases get all supernatural.

8

Raging Bullfrog

Mr. Ratnose was no fool. Rather than ride herd on a class of unruly students, he packed us off to Coach Beef Stroganoff for a double dose of torture—also known as P.E. class.

Not that I have anything against exercise. I could sit and watch other kids do it all day. But Coach takes exercise seriously.

He ran us, ragged on us, and worked us out. By the time school ended, I was just a puddle of sweat with a hat on it.

Natalie found me propped up against the flagpole, half conscious.

"Ready for some detecting?" she chirped.

"Ready for a bath and a nap," I said, "maybe at the same time."

Natalie punched my shoulder. "Come on, Chet, we've got a suspect to interview. Get the lead out."

I groaned and levered myself upright. "Funny, that's what Coach Stroganoff said. But now my legs are full of it."

By the time Natalie and I walked the five long blocks to Albert Dentay's house, I felt just fine. Like the newspaper at the bottom of a parakeet cage.

"You gotta get more exercise," Natalie said, waiting for me to draw near.

"Either that, or a pair of robot legs. Maybe Dr. Lightov can fix me up."

We reached the corner of Whippoorwill Lane, and I checked the address I'd copied from the phone book. "There's our guy," I said.

Two doors down, a brawny bullfrog was puttering in his yard.

Natalie grabbed my arm. "So who are we?"

"Chet and Natalie, birdbrain. Who did you think?"

"No, we need a cover," she said. "Who are we pretending to be?"

"Um, circus freaks?"

She shook her head. "Newspaper reporters." Natalie slipped on a pair of glasses. I turned up my hat brim, and fished a pencil and some paper from my pocket.

We approached the bullfrog, who was hacking his hedge with a vengeance. Thick, ropy muscles danced beneath his olive green skin like baby snakes doing the mambo. His frown was wide and deep enough to swallow Cuba, with a little room left over for Buenos Aires.

To top it off, the frog wore a white chef's hat. For doing his yardwork.

I cleared my throat. "Are you Albert Dentay?"

He sized us up with a pop-eyed stare. "Yeah?"

"We're from the school paper, y'know," said Natalie in her best airhead voice. "And we're, like, totally reporting on the new machines at school."

"Got time for a few questions?" I asked.

"Unh," grunted Al. I took that for a yes.

Natalie asked, "So, like, when did the Munchmeister 2000 start up?"

"Yesterday," he rumbled.

"And you were fired today?" I asked.

Just then, a horsefly buzzed between us. We both locked eyes on the treat.

Tha-zzzip! My tongue shot out and snagged the fly.

That's me, Quick-Draw McGecko.

Al scowled at me. He scowled at the grass. Then he picked up a hedge trimmer and turned it on with a deafening *blaaaahht*.

Oh, great. A sore loser.

Natalie shot me a look that said, *What did you do that for?*

I sent her a look that said, *Because I was hungry. Duh.*

The bullfrog butchered some shrubbery. Natalie plastered on a smile and broke out the girlish charm, resting her wing tip on his forearm.

Al turned off his gizmo. My hearing returned.

"We, like, weren't totally finished," said Natalie.

"So you got laid off?" I said. "Where were you just before lunch?"

"Home," he grunted. Mr. Dentay reached for the starter button.

Natalie leaned in, batting her eyes. "That's totally gnarly, your being laid off," she said. "Like, share how that makes you feel."

The bullfrog's frown deepened. "Bad," he croaked.

Man, this guy was a regular Mr. Chatty. I wondered what it would take to squeeze a whole sentence out of him.

I decided to try. "Is it true you'd do almost anything to get your job back?"

The ex-chef's jaws clamped down hard. His finger jabbed the hedge trimmer's starter button.

Blah-blaaaaahhht roared the tool.

Mr. Dentay bent and massacred something green at the edge of his immaculate lawn.

I leaned closer, shouting, "Did you put something funny into the school lunch?"

The bullfrog's head came up. His pop eyes blazed.

"No!" he bellowed.

Natalie shouted, "Just one more que—"

Bra-BRAHHHHT! Mr. Dentay shifted the trimmer into high gear and swung it at us like a samurai sword.

"No"—*swipe!*—"more"—*swipe!*—"questions!"

We jumped backward, dodging the deadly blades.

Al Dentay hopped after us, repeating his war cry. "No! More! *Questions!*"

Natalie and I turned and fled down the street. Freaky frog gave up at the corner, but we didn't slow down for another half block.

At last we stopped to catch our breath. I looked over at Natalie.

"It takes a lot for him to open up," I said. "But boy, once you get him talking, that Al is a real blabbermouth."

After a close call, nothing calms the nerves like some katydid crisp bars and a cool glass of mantis milk. Natalie and I carried our snack to my backyard office, cleverly disguised as a refrigerator box.

Neither of us said a thing until the last crisp was crunched.

Then I belched and patted my gut.

Natalie put her wing tips together and frowned.

"What do you—?" we both began.

I held out a hand. "Lady birds first."

"What do you think about our suspects?" she said.

"Beats me. The witches might have the know-how to turn kids loco. But what's their motive?"

Natalie nodded. "And Al Dentay had motive but no access."

"At least not today." I stifled another belch.

"Dr. Lightov also had the chance to fiddle with that food," Natalie said.

"*If* the food is what's making kids flip. But from what I overheard, she seems to want to *control* students, not make 'em go wild."

"Hmm," she said.

"Hmm," I agreed.

The breeze sighed outside our box. The faint chatter of the TV drifted from my house.

"Brain break?" I said.

"It's the wise move," Natalie said.

I led the way back inside. "As a smart detective once said, he who hits a dead end should regroup and watch cartoons."

"'Smart detective'?" she squawked. "Chet, *you* said that."

"What, I'm not a smart detective?"

She grinned. "Smart *aleck,* maybe."

9

Nobody Does It Badger

The next day dawned cloudy with a chance of mystery. My thoughts weren't any clearer than the night before, but I hit school early anyhow. Maybe a little snooping would turn up something.

Or not. But a gecko's got to try.

It was one of those gray mornings where everything seems to move in slow motion. A crossing guard leaned on a lamppost, waiting for crossers to show up. A handful of kids dawdled by the office.

I turned my toes toward the cafeteria. An alert detective might pick up some clues there (or at least a stray sow-bug muffin).

But just as I rounded the corner of the building, a great chunk of the wall stepped into my path.

"Hold it right there," said the wall.

I noticed it was covered with bristly gray-and-black fur. Odd, for a wall. Tilting my head back, I looked up, up, up...into the inky eyes of a badger.

"Right there?" I said. "But I'd rather hold it over here." Quick as a scalded monkey, I feinted left and dodged right—right into the badger's massive paw.

"I want you should listen," growled the badger, grinding my shoulder into raw flyburger.

"Ow!" I squinted up at her.

The badger's snout was trained on me like a booger cannon. One white fang twinkled in the corner of her mouth. How did I know this monster was a *she*? The pink headband and golden heart locket were dead giveaways.

"I listen better when my shoulder isn't being mangled," I said.

"Who doesn't," said Goldie Locket, giving my shoulder another friendly squeeze—friendly like a python's hug. "You're investigating a case, yes?"

"Yes."

She leaned down, nose to nose. I turned my head against the assault of her onion-and-liverwurst breath.

"Don't," she said.

"Don't what?" I asked.

"Don't investigate."

I tried a chuckle. "It's what I do. Fish gotta swim, detectives gotta detect."

Goldie Locket growled. The paw tightened on my shoulder until I could almost feel the claws meet.

"Ow, ow, ow!"

"This isn't career counseling, shamus. It's health advice."

"Health advice?" I said.

"Yeah. You wanna go on living, yes?" Goldie asked.

I cocked my head. "Depends on my other choices."

The badger turned uglier than a plate of broccoli at breakfast. "My friend, he doesn't like your snooping. You keep it up, you're gonna find out."

Goldie straightened, effortlessly lifting me. "It's a small school, Gecko," she said. "But there's a hundred places a PI could get lost and never be seen again."

In a swift move, the badger cocked me over her shoulder and hurled me onto the roof of the cafeteria.

I crawled to the edge and looked down at her. "You know, the football team could use a good man like you," I said. Just to show her that being tossed around doesn't throw me.

In a voice as sincere as an undertaker's get-well

card, Goldie said, "You take care, shamus." Then she lumbered off down the hall.

After a start like that, my day had nowhere to go but up.

But strangely enough, it didn't.

Mrs. Bagoong was busy turning hot dogs into Munchmeister gloop. No muffins in sight. Reminding her to watch out for conspirators, I moved on.

I stopped by the scrofulous tree, on the chance Natalie might turn up.

She didn't.

When the five-minute bell rang, I strolled to my room, thinking deep, detective-y thoughts. Like, who was the badger's mysterious friend? And why didn't he want me on the case? I passed a small knot of girls.

A field mouse giggled. "And here you are again. Following us?"

Her friends giggled, too.

I shook my head. "Not if you were an ice-cream truck with the last chocolate-coated banana slug in the world. Where was I before?"

"Over by the library, silly," said the mouse. The whine of a nearby machine almost drowned her out.

"Ooh, Gecko's got it bad!" said her friend, a spiky-haired shrew.

Was I that distracted? I didn't even remember passing the library or seeing these little cootie monsters before.

I would have mulled it further, but my train of thought was suddenly derailed by a loud *greee-aanngh!*

The Yard Czar rumbled past, sucking up leaves. Maureen DeBree waved from the driver's seat. She seemed to be in much better control of the equipment now.

Or not.

With a crunch like a giant snacking on moose antlers, the machine shook and shimmied. And suddenly—*pftahhh!*—it burped out leaves and grass clippings in a fountain of green.

This might have been funny. If the fountain wasn't spewing at me.

"Eeee!" squealed the girls, scattering.

I raised my arms for protection. Too late. Grass flew in my eyes, my nose, my mouth, and down my shirt. *"Pt-thpt-pft!"* I backed off, spitting shredded greens.

The girls giggled. Big surprise there.

"Sorry, eh!" Ms. DeBree turned a key. The leaf-spitting brute gave a few last gasps and shut off. "Confunit!" she cried, hitting the steering wheel. "This contraption is nothing but trouble!"

"You're telling me," I said.

"First, I gotta fire my assistant. Then they stick me with this junk thing!"

My detective radar went off. "You fired your assistant?"

Ms. DeBree shook her furry noggin. "Emmanuel Laber," she said. "Shoots, and I just trained the guy. The machine took his place."

"Was he sore?"

"Hoo! Like some Tanzanian dribble."

I hid a smile. "You mean, Tasmanian devil?"

And with that the class bell rang. Much as I wanted to pursue that promising lead, it was time to go pretend to learn something until I was free to investigate again.

School, *schmool*. This was one heck of a way to run a detective agency.

10

Between a Doc and a Hard Place

I puzzled through Mr. Ratnose's lesson, trying to make the pieces fit. No, not the pieces of his lesson— the pieces of my case. It struck me that the fired staff might have good reason for sabotaging Dr. Lightov's inventions.

But how were they doing it? Both Mr. Dentay and Mr. Laber had been booted off the school grounds. Did they have an accomplice on the inside?

The sound of my name broke into my thoughts.

"Chet Gecko, what do we get when we total these numbers on the board?"

I glanced up at my teacher. "Mr. Ratnose, there are three types of mathematicians: those who can add, and those who can't."

He clenched his jaw and shook his head. I actually

felt a little sorry for the guy. But he should know better than to interrupt me when I'm working.

I pondered on.

My classmates seemed no goofier than usual this morning. In fact, Bitty Chu and Igor Beaver were back to being apple-polishing teacher's pets.

Fat lot of good it did them. As Igor told me just before breaktime, they'd both been kicked off the math team.

He passed me a quarter. "That's for all your hard work," he said. "But I guess I don't um, need you anymore."

I pocketed the coin.

Recess came, and with it a surge of new energy. A smile twisted my lips. I would get to the bottom of this mystery.

No matter that I had no client. No matter that I had more suspects than fingers. I would prevail.

Natalie and I met up in the hallway as kids streamed past.

"Hey, I've been thinking," I said.

"Careful," she said, "it's tricky your first time out."

I took her wing and steered her out of the traffic flow. "What if all this fuss was some revenge scheme cooked up by the staff who got fired?"

Natalie cocked her head. "You think they might have it in for Dr. Lightov?"

64

"One way to find out. Let's talk to the good doctor herself."

Natalie smiled. "I'm your bird."

We caught up with the inventor in the library. Tanya Lightov stood on a chair by the Bibliomalgamator. Its top was off, her sleeves were rolled up, and she was poking about inside with a wrench. Black oil smudged her furry cheeks.

"What's up, doc?" I said as we approached.

"Oh, zhis machine," she said, waving the wrench. *"Grrr!"* She followed this with a few choice phrases in Russian.

I could only assume they were phrases not meant for a kid's ears.

At his desk, Cool Beans looked up from scanning books and shushed her. She sneered back.

"Got a minute?" I asked.

The woodchuck's icy gaze dismissed us. "I am busy scientist. No time to vaste vith children."

"We're, uh, from the yearbook," said Natalie. She gave me the eye.

"Uh, that's right," I said. "Want to say something for the record?"

You could tell the groundhog was impressed by our bogus credentials. She puffed up like a bouncy castle at a birthday party.

"For history? *Da,* I have two minutes. Speak."

Natalie cleared her throat. "Well, your project is, um, very impressive."

"Naturally," said the woodchuck. "Is my project."

"Why did you choose it?" asked Natalie.

"Vhy? Zhis school is run by morons, losing money. I can help."

I produced a pencil and paper, to look more writerly. Doodling a dinosaur, I said, "And what about the students? How do you feel about them?"

She brushed her whiskers with the back of a paw. "*Pffft,* children," she said. "If I run zhis place, children vould behave much better—like nice little robots."

Natalie and I exchanged a glance.

"I bet not everyone appreciates your brilliance," said Natalie.

She was laying it on a bit thick. But the woodchuck smiled.

"Precisely," she said. "Ze administration resists my best ideas, like putting ze microchips in students. Staff are jealous."

"Your machines put some guys out of work," I said. "Do you think they might try sabotage?"

Dr. Lightov's eyebrows drew together like two caterpillars dancing the tango. "You think sabotage?" she said.

"Could be," said Natalie. "Anyone in particular come to mind?"

The inventor's blue laser gaze rested on Cool Beans for a long moment.

"I cannot say," she said. "Now leave me. I must vork."

We said our good-byes and beat feet. As we left, the groundhog was muttering to herself, tinkering with her invention, and shooting evil looks at the librarian.

As we stepped outside, I said, "Do you really believe Cool Beans would...?"

"Never in a million years," Natalie said.

We stood on the top step and blinked in the bright sunshine. The jolly cries of kids at play echoed around us. It all seemed so normal.

It was anything but.

"You know," said Natalie, "what if Dr. Lightov herself did the sabotage?"

I looked over at her. "That again? Come on."

Natalie hopped down the steps. "Hear me out. She said she wanted to put microchips into kids to control us."

"Yeah, so?" I followed her onto the walkway.

"What better way to kick off that plan than with students going crazy?"

"Hmm," I said, seeing her point. "Create the problem..."

"And then offer the solution."

I clapped her on the shoulder. "Partner, you might be onto something."

She grinned. "So what now, Mr. PI?"

I scratched my head and looked out at the playground. Too many choices.

"Um . . . ," I began.

Natalie smirked. "What say we stake out the cafeteria at lunch and try to catch the culprit in the act?"

"Now why didn't I think of that?"

"Because I thought of it first?" she said.

Taking Natalie by the wing, I made a beeline for the snack machine in the hallway. "This calls for a treat," I said.

"How generous," said Natalie.

I stopped in front of it. "Yes, you are. So why don't you treat me to a Pillbug Crunch bar?"

11

Till Death Do Us Partner

Back in class the minutes limped by like a millipede with blisters. Our lessons seemed to take forever, but at last, history class was history.

It was time to detect.

Wading into the happy chaos of kids bound for lunch, I picked up the pace. Natalie and I had planned to meet by the cafeteria door. We had to move fast if we wanted to catch our culprit. (So fast, I would have to eat lunch later. Nobody appreciates the sacrifices we private eyes make.)

But before I got halfway to the lunchroom, a high-pitched shrilling like the buzz of giant mosquitoes distracted me. I turned, searching the skies.

The sound swelled.

Wham! Something slammed into me at waist level.

I went down hard, like a steel-belted birthday cake. Little bodies swarmed. Little feet trampled over me. Little voices shouted, "Yaaahh! We rule!"

I tucked and rolled to the side. Rising carefully into a crouch, I turned to see what evil force had attacked me.

Kindergartners?

A whole class of them swept by, just finished with early lunch.

I shook my head.

This made no sense. In the school pecking order, kindergartners occupied the bottom rung. They were supposed to be cute. They were supposed to be shy. But savage? Never.

The little thugs shoved past fourth and fifth graders with no regard for life and limb. And then, in a twitch of a rat's tail, they were gone.

Standing upright, I dusted myself off. Here was a mystery. Could it be linked to my case?

Getting my tail in gear, I hustled over to the cafeteria. But by the time I reached it, the Munchmeister 2000 was cranking out food, and kids were lining up.

I checked out their lunches—gross and gloopy as ever. Whether it was spiked with loco juice or not, the food was seriously funky.

"Yuck," I said. "Who would eat that stuff?"

"Plenty of people," said a nearby kid.

I glanced at the line, but didn't see the speaker. "Who said that?"

Pete Moss waved his hand in front of my face. "Hello? Me again."

"Oh, Pete, I—"

"Did not see me, I know." He scowled. "Nobody does."

"Sorry, Ace. No time to sit and jaw. I'm on a case."

Mrs. Bagoong was working back in the kitchen. I buttonholed her.

"So what's the story, Brown Eyes?" I asked.

"Oh," she said, looking up from rinsing trays. "Hello, Chet honey."

"Did you catch anyone messing with the machine?"

Her eyebrow ridges drew together. "Why, no. It's been so busy . . ."

I stepped closer. "Think. Was anyone unusual hanging around right before lunch?"

The big iguana stroked her scaly chin. "Let's see . . . Mr. Zero stopped in . . . That inventor was here, adjusting things. And some older kid came by, looking for her little brother."

"Older kid?" I asked. "What did she look like?"

Mrs. Bagoong ruffled the spikes on her head.

"Let's see . . . a tall, skinny alligator lizard. Wearing a purple, flowered T-shirt."

Could it be the bad-tempered Miss Purple Tee?

"Hmm," I said.

"What does that mean?" she asked.

"It means . . . hmm. Unless I miss my guess, that lizard is one of the witches."

The lunch lady frowned. "Which witches?"

"That's right," I said. "*Witch* witches."

Mrs. Bagoong gave me an odd look. "I just had the strangest sense of déjà vu."

"Me, too, sister. All over again." I turned and hustled out of the lunchroom.

Curses or no curses, it was time to take another look at those witches. I could sure use Natalie's help. Where was that mockingbird?

"Natalie!" I spotted her down the hall.

My partner narrowed her eyes and turned away. I hurried after her. "Hey, didn't you hear me?"

Over her shoulder, Natalie shot me a look that was colder than a polar bear's pizza.

"Partner, what's wrong?" I asked, catching up.

Natalie spun. "Like you don't know," she snapped.

"But I don't."

She bristled and addressed two passing girls. "Oh, right. The great detective has no idea why his part-ner might be mad at him."

They gave her a sympathetic look and moved along.

"I've got no clue," I said. "Snap out of this—we've got work to do."

"*We've* got work? *We've?*" The fire in Natalie's eyes nearly set my hat aflame. "After what you said, you expect me to help solve your dumb case?"

My face flushed. "What in the world has gotten into you?"

Natalie thrust her beak close. "Into *me*?" she said. "You've been shooting down my ideas for days. Then, just five minutes ago, you said I was deadweight and a lousy detective and you'd be better off without me."

"What?" I felt like I'd been smacked in the face with a wet slug. "You're loco!"

Natalie stabbed a forefeather in my face. "Darn right, I'm crazy. Crazy to think you were my friend!"

Her brown eyes welled up.

"Natalie, I—"

"No more!" she said. "I'm outta here!" And she flapped her wings and took off.

"Wait, I was in the lunchroom five minutes ago!" I called after her. "Natalie!"

But she was gone, long gone, like last summer's melted Popsicles.

12

Par for the Curse

I paced. This was goofier than a carload of circus chimps on a banana binge. Was Natalie going cuckoo, or was I?

What could make a person act so strangely?

Then it hit me: a spell. Natalie was under a *spell*!

Geckos may be cold-blooded, but I swear mine ran hot right then. I clenched my fists. If those witches thought they could mess with my partner, they had another think coming.

Their bums were gum, and I was the chewer.

I hightailed it across the playground, making for the yew tree. This gecko was going to get some answers.

But when I reached the shade of the evergreen, there wasn't a witch in sight.

"Gnarrgh!" I snarled. I kicked the white stones from their witchy circle, sending them into the bushes.

"Hey!" cried a voice.

The alligator lizard in the purple T-shirt, the green-spotted toad, and the tabby kitten stood at the edge of the grass.

"What are you doing?" said the cat.

I stomped toward them. "Breaking up your little crime ring, that's what."

"You're barking up the wrong tree, buster," said Purple Tee.

"You'd like me to think so, wouldn't you?" I said, shaking a finger in her face. "You hexed my partner, and you're dropping wacky dust in the food to make kids nuts. Well, it's not gonna work."

"What's not?" said the toad. "The nuts?"

"Your evil plan, Spotty. You witches have cast your last curse."

Purple Tee glowered down at me. "Watch your step, Gecko."

I gave her glare for glare. "Funny, bad guys have been telling me that for years. But I just keep on stepping."

Spotty pulled on the lizard's arm. "Becca," she said warningly.

"No," said Becca. "I've had enough of these dummies giving Wicca a bad name, calling us witches."

"You're worried about your good name?" I said. "Should've thought of that before you started doing your evil hoodoo."

"Hoodoo?" sputtered the lizard. "*Hoo*doo?"

"*You* do," I said. "That's who."

"Enough!" Becca cried. "We're hexing this gecko."

I drew myself up. "Just try it, Becky-Baby. I'm gonna get the evidence to send you witches straight down the drain."

Becca turned away to rebuild the circle of stones. The kitten hissed.

Spotty shrugged. "Sorry. She did warn you."

"I'm not afraid of you," I said.

The lizard looked up. "You should be, PI."

"Oh, yeah? Why's that?"

"If you don't catch the real culprit by noon tomorrow, you'll be seeing the world from a very different point of view—a worm's-eye view."

I planted my hands on my hips. "No worries, witchie-poo. I'll catch you red-handed by then."

But Becca just started humming a curious tune. She sat inside her circle and reached out for the cat and toad, who joined her.

Together they held hands and sang:

"Spin the circle round and round
Call the freaky powers down
Strike the gecko, though he squirm
Turn him into crawly worm—"

I backed away. "This isn't over. Principal Zero is gonna shut you nutjobs down." When I reached the grass, I turned and stalked off, shoulders squared.

But inside me, a larva of doubt wriggled.

They were nutjobs, no question. But did these nutjobs have the power to turn a PI into a pink night crawler?

Though I searched the school, I couldn't find Natalie anywhere. So when the bell rang, I shuffled back to class. Just down the hall from my room, a long, curly tail shot out from behind a corner, blocking my path.

"Not so fast, Romeo," said a breathy voice.

It was Shirley Chameleon. She batted her bulging eyes.

"The name's Gecko," I said. "You must have me confused with someone."

She giggled. "Where did you run off to, Chet?"

I tugged on my hat. "Run off? I've been working a case."

Shirley's tail curled around my legs and tugged. I stumbled toward her.

She put a hand on my chest. "You think you can just kiss a girl like that and walk away?"

"What are you babbling about?" I said. "I only kiss relatives—and then, only at gunpoint."

Shirley's tail tugged again. We were nose to nose. "That's not the song you were singing a little while ago," she crooned. "Now, give me some more of that sugar, sugar."

Her eyes half closed, Shirley pooched up her lips and leaned forward.

Alarms clanged in my brain: *Danger! Danger!*

I broke free and shoved her away. "Back off, you dizzy dame!"

Hurt filled her eyes like the gooey center of chocolate-covered chigger mites. "But Chet, you promised me another kiss."

"Not on a million-dollar bet, sister," I said, and scooted down the hall. Sprinting through the classroom door, I slipped into my seat. Had the whole school gone bonkers?

I didn't know for sure. But I did know that when I caught those witches in the act, they would pay for what they'd done.

Bad enough that they'd bewitched the school and hexed my partner.

But turning me into a cootie magnet?

That's something that this gecko will *never* put up with.

13

The Surreal Deal

All through lessons, Shirley kept making goo-goo eyes. I ignored her.

Fortunately, the class was acting crankier than a cave full of grizzlies startled out of hibernation. With this as a cover, I ate my sack lunch in peace.

Before the first hour was over, Mr. Ratnose had sent seven more kids to the principal's office. Add this to the seven kids who'd been suspended yesterday, and that put our class at half strength. (Even I could do this kind of math.)

A few more days, and I'd be the last one standing, with Mr. Ratnose as my private tutor. A scary thought.

I made a vow to never let it get that far.

When the bell announced late recess, I shot from my seat like snow peas flung from a spoon. My first priority: patching things up with Natalie. No matter what spell she was under, my partner would eventually listen to reason.

I hoped.

Frantically, I checked the usual spots—scrofulous tree, library, and swings.

No Natalie. Man, she must *really* be sore.

Since my partner was in hiding, I switched to my second priority: proving to Mr. Zero that the witches were behind all the trouble at school. I needed evidence. Maybe if I shadowed them and caught them with their hands in the cookie jar?

Acting casual, I ambled over to the portable buildings—the perfect place to eyeball the yew tree and pick up their trail. Or so I thought.

I should have known. Nothing is ever perfect for this gecko.

Just past the last portable, something big blocked the sun. A solar eclipse? I wish. It was my old friend Goldie Locket, the badger.

A paw big enough to seat three kindergartners swept down from the sky and grabbed my shirtfront.

"What did I tell you?" said the badger.

"Look both ways when crossing the street, and brush after every meal?"

She growled. "How can one little gecko cause so much trouble?"

"Just lucky, I guess."

Goldie Locket lifted me off my feet. "I try to warn him," she said. "I try to be Ms. Nice Guy, and this is the thanks I get?"

"Uh, who are you talking to?" I asked.

"You, shamus," she snarled. "I want you should stop sticking your nose into things."

I tried to pry her paw from my shirt. It was like trying to crack a safe with a bendy straw.

"But since I'm not getting through," said the badger, "maybe I should do something to *really* get your attention, yes?"

"That's not necessary," I said.

Goldie's other fist drew back, as big and gray as a rogue asteroid. I could tell it was about to crash into the moon of my face.

Unless help came quickly, my handsome mug would be ruined. I did the first thing I could think of. I bit her paw.

"Ow!" Goldie Locket dropped me like a bad habit.

And speaking of bad, who should show up at that moment but the biggest, baddest cat at school?

"Mr. Zero!" I cried. "Man, am I happy to see you."

"Not half as happy as I am," the principal purred.

I pointed at Goldie Locket. "This goon was about to make mincemeat out of my face."

She froze.

"Really?" said Mr. Zero.

"Yup." I glared at the badger. She was in for it now.

The big cat chuckled. "Seems only fair."

"Huh?" I said.

"After the way you beat up three kids and sent them to the nurse's office, that seems like a fair punishment," said Principal Zero.

I spluttered. "B-but I never—"

Goldie Locket smiled. Her white fangs sparkled.

Mr. Zero held up a paw. "Save it," he said. "A playground full of witnesses saw you. You're a first-class troublemaker."

The badger held up her paw. "He bit me," she said.

"I'm not surprised," said Mr. Zero. "But don't worry. He'll pay."

The principal's huge paw clamped around my upper arm. "Come along, Gecko. I've been too easy on you for too long. But not anymore."

"What do you mean?" I asked.

Mr. Zero led me away. "This time, I'm throwing the book at you."

"If you like, I should be glad to testify," the badger called after us.

The big cat hustled me across the grass. Kids stopped playing and stared.

"What are you going to do?" I asked.

"This school, as you know very well, has a zero-tolerance rule on fighting," he rumbled. "One strike and you're out."

My eyes went wide. "But you can't..."

"I've already called your mother. You, Gecko, are suspended from school."

Ice water filled my veins. "Suspended?" I croaked.

"For the rest of the week," said the principal.

I was flabbergasted, bug-eyed, and boggled. My tongue was soggy newspaper, and my legs were linguini. As Mr. Zero dragged me off, one thought kept running through my mind like Chicken Little at a meteor shower.

I was suspended.

And then a second thought followed: If I was suspended, how the heck was I supposed to patch things up with Natalie and solve the case?

The third, cruelest thought told me: If I didn't solve the case, the witches' curse would come true.

And I knew what that meant.

Good-bye, Gecko. Hello, Worm Boy.

14

Undivided Suspension

Blue doesn't even come close to describing my mood that afternoon. Kids sent to bed without supper are blue. I was gloom-founded, hurtin' for certain, down in the Dumpster, majorly mope-ified.

I was the poster boy of bummers.

For an hour at home I grumped and whined. For another hour I moaned and drooped. I eyed the dirt outside the window. I thought about eating it, to get a head start on my wormhood.

Nothing could penetrate my funk.

Finally, I lay on the sofa, staring into space. There was no way around it. This time Chet Gecko was going down for good.

A face appeared above me. An upside-down gecko, my little sister, Pinky.

"Wass wrong, big brother?" she said.

"You wouldn't understand." I heaved a sigh and rolled onto my side. "Only Natalie could help me puzzle through this, and she's not talking to me."

"Okay," said Pinky.

Plucking at a loose thread on the cushion, I said, "I was kicked out of school for doing something I didn't do. And now my life is over."

"But you didn' do it?" she said, coming around to the front of the couch.

"No."

Pinky frowned. "Huh. Sounds like a mystery."

She wandered off to the kitchen. I stared at the spot where she'd been standing.

A mystery? It sure as heck *was* a mystery. *And what did Chet Gecko do with mysteries?* I asked myself.

"Solve them," I said out loud.

Sure, I'd been kicked out of school. And sure, I'd be turning into a worm at noon tomorrow.

But this gecko had *never* turned his back on a mystery.

I sat up. If you're going to go down, might as well go down swinging.

Somehow the witches had tricked my partner into believing I hated her, made Shirley Chameleon think that I *liked* her, and convinced a bunch of kids that I was a slug-happy bully. But how?

Hopping to my feet, I began to pace.

First things first. I couldn't solve this without my partner. So somehow I'd have to talk Natalie into—if not being my friend—at least helping me out.

I reached for the phone.

"Hello? Attired residence," came her familiar voice.

"Natalie, please don't hang up," I said.

She hung up.

I called back. "I asked you not to hang up."

"Like I'd do anything *you* asked me to," she said.

"Please, partner. I need you." I twisted the phone cord in my fingers.

She squawked. "Oh, *now* he needs me."

Pacing again, I continued. "I do. Remember when I was framed for stealing food? And when I was framed for kidnapping that penguin?"

"Good times," said Natalie.

89

"Well, I'm being framed again. Whatever you think I said to you, I didn't say it."

"Sure."

"Natalie, I can't crack this case without your help. Please?"

The silence stretched like a giraffe doing yoga. I heard her breath. I held my own.

"If I get even the slightest hint that you *aren't* being framed...," she said.

"Lock me up and throw away the key."

She paused again. "This doesn't mean I forgive you. You are going to owe me *big-time*."

A strange knot choked my throat. Probably the wolf spider quesadillas I'd eaten earlier.

"Thanks, partner."

"We'll see," she said.

The next morning, I acted the part of the heart-break kid. I lingered in bed. I moped over my dragon-fly flakes. I dawdled over my homework (actually, that part wasn't acting).

In short, I did everything possible to reassure my mom that this gecko was going to grump around the house all day.

Still, when she headed to work at 10:30, Ma Gecko issued a warning: "If I find out you've left the house for any reason while I'm gone, you are grounded, mister."

No fool, my mother.

As I watched her go, I mulled it over. True, if I went to school I'd probably be grounded. But since I'd be a worm if I didn't solve this case, I'd be grounded if I *didn't* go—and permanently.

I decided to stick with the plan.

Waiting a few minutes to make sure my mom was really gone, I slipped out the door and hotfooted it down the street. The neighborhood was quiet—kids at school, parents at work. I felt as conspicuous as a tarantula on a dinner plate.

My feet slowed as I neared Emerson Hicky. It would take some major sneakiness to avoid Mrs. Crow's eagle eye. (Or should that be *crow* eye?)

I scoped out the school gate. All clear. I checked out the office windows. Blurry shapes passed inside—too risky.

Crouching low, I scooted across the street and made for a shaggy oak tree by the fence. So far, so good. With a last look-see for stray teachers, I scrambled up the tree and out onto a limb.

For a moment I dangled at arm's length, then dropped like an overripe fruit.

Whump! The grass broke my fall. I was in!

"Nice drop," came a scratchy voice.

In trouble.

15

Snare and Snare Alike

I whirled to face my captor.

"Why you never come through the gate?" asked the mongoose.

"Ms. DeBree!" I cried. Would she turn me in? Maybe the custodian hadn't heard about my suspension. "Oh, uh, I'm undercover."

She surveyed the wide expanse of grass. "Not much cover, if you ask me. Where you headed?"

"The cafeteria."

Ms. DeBree flipped back the lid of her rolling rubbish bin. "Hop in," she said.

"What happened to the Yard Czar?" I eyed the bin.

The custodian shook her head. "Chee whiz, the

frikkedy thing keeps breaking down." She patted the bin. "The old ways is best."

I climbed into the oversized plastic trash container. It reeked of spoiled food, sour milk, and something even fouler. I coughed.

"Sorry, eh?" said Ms. DeBree. "Shoulda warned you. Some kindergartner had an accident."

"*Now* you tell me." I pinched my nose and cracked the lid for fresh air.

The cafeteria lay just down the hill. It couldn't come soon enough.

After my brief but breathless ride, the custodian dropped me off behind the building. I hopped out.

"Just one second," she said. "I heard you was suspended."

Busted. I turned up my palms. "Uh, you see . . ."

"But I never believed it," she said. "Good luck, Mr. Private Eyeball." Ms. DeBree trundled off.

I blew out a sigh. Now, to solve a mystery.

The cafeteria's side door led backstage. (Yes, our cafeteria doubles as an auditorium. Blame it on the school's cheapskate first principal.) Climbing the wooden steps, I found myself in the dimness behind the red velvet curtain.

Earlier this morning, Natalie had planted notes with all of our suspects, from the most likely (witches), to the least likely (Dr. Lightov), to the completely unlikable (Al Dentay). The message was simple and anonymous:

> I'VE GOT PROOF THAT YOU DID IT.
> MEET ME BACKSTAGE AT 11 A.M.
> WITH A BAG OF MONEY. WE'LL TRADE.

By now, everyone knew I'd been suspended (except maybe Mr. Dentay). So they wouldn't be expecting me there.

I groped around inside a big box of erasers. My fingers closed on cool metal. Good ol' Natalie. She had stashed her brother's camera, so I could capture the crook on film.

Turning the camera on, I leaned against the wall to wait. It didn't take long.

Footsteps echoed outside. The door creaked open, and the culprit stood revealed in a wash of daylight.

I leaped forward and snapped off a shot. "Got you red-handed, you witch!"

Dr. Tanya Lightov raised a paw against the flash's glare. "Zhese are strong vords," she said. "Maybe I am bad lady, but I am still lady."

My mouth fell open. "You? *You* made those kids go nuts? You fooled my partner and framed me?"

The woodchuck frowned. "Eh?" she said. "I don't know vhat you speak of."

94

"Then vhy—I mean, why are you here?"

She clutched a brown bag to her lab coat. "Don't toy vith me. You know vhy. Now give me ze proof, and I give you money."

It was my turn to frown. "But I—"

"You cruel child," she said. "You vant me to say it? Okay, I say it: I copied ze inventions of my brother, Ivan."

"Huh?"

The inventor hung her shaggy head. "I am not proud. But I needed zhis job, so I borrowed his ideas. I am bad, bad sister."

"Um, that's really rotten and all," I said, "but that's not the crime I had in mind."

Dr. Lightov's head came up. "Vhat?"

"Keep your money. I'm after whoever hexed those kids and got me thrown out of school."

"You have no *proof*?" The groundhog's eyes lit up like a volcano project at Science Fair. "Ha! Zhen everyzhing I just tell you is a lie. I never stole my brother's ideas." She shook the brown bag. "Zhis? Zhis is my lunch!"

And with that, the inventor parted the curtains, hopped off the stage, and skedaddled through the cafeteria.

I stood flat-footed, staring after her. So, Dr. Lightov wasn't the culprit.

Then who was?

At that, the side door banged open. "Me!" cried a voice.

A shortish figure stood haloed in the bright sunshine. It wore a coat and hat, and seemed awfully familiar.

I squinted.

Green skin. Long lizard tail. Slight gut. Detective-y hat. Handsome face.

It was like looking in a mirror.

A wave of wooziness swept me, like army ants crawling up my body—from the inside. But this was no mirror; this was my exact double!

I stumbled back a step.

"It was me," said the fake Chet Gecko. "I did it!"

16

Double Whammy

If you've ever stood up too fast and gotten light-headed, you might have some slight idea of how I felt—if you multiplied the effect by about a million.

My head spun like a dizzy dame in a shampoo commercial. My legs wobbled. My brain was a soggy bowl of mantis mush.

"What?" I said. "How?"

I stared at the *other* Chet Gecko. Every detail was perfect, from the battered fedora, to the striped T-shirt, to the jaunty curve in the tail.

The sheer impossibility of it staggered me.

Strangely, the first thing I thought was, *Man, this is going to bug Mr. Ratnose.*

Pull it together, Chet. *Focus.*

"How is this even possible?" I said.

"I am the guilty one," said the bogus Chet Gecko in a stiff voice. He held out a bag. "Here is the loot, Jack. Just do not rat me out."

I sniffed. *Loot? Rat me out?* Sure this guy looked like me, but he didn't sound a *thing* like me. Natalie and Shirley must have been deaf not to catch it.

Moving closer, I noticed that his skin seemed a little too perfect and his movements a little too awkward. "Who the heck are you?" I said.

"I am Chet Gecko," he said.

I clattered down the steps to stand beside the impostor.

His head swiveled to watch me, whirring faintly.

I touched his cheek. Cold. But not lizard-skin cold, metal-cold.

"A robot," I muttered. Somebody had built a scary-good Chet Gecko robot.

The creature's eyes flashed. "What?" it said. "Who is this?"

"I'm the *real* Chet Gecko, you bucket of junk!"

I reached for the impostor, but it swung the sack and clocked me, hard.

Whonk! The bag must have held concrete, kryptonite, and rolls of quarters.

Down I went like a skydiving elephant. The steps crunched into my back.

"Oooh." I slowly sat up, holding my throbbing cheek.

The door was closing. The robot had hightailed it.

"Hey!" I cried. "I'm not done with you, mister!"

Struggling to my feet, I pushed outside. A green tail was disappearing around the building.

I dashed in pursuit. Just past the corner, a mob of first graders was piling into the lunchroom. No sign of the robot.

"Hey, did you guys see a green gecko?" I asked.

"Right here," said a rat, looking at me.

"Besides me," I said.

A little porcupine stared up, big-eyed. "Yeah. You went thataway." She pointed down the hall.

As I hit the next corridor, I spotted the robot to my left. Dang, that droid was fast. But I was faster.

I made like a bakery truck and hauled buns. We passed one building, two buildings. Stride by stride, I gained ground.

Then, up ahead of Fake Chet, I saw someone else running—someone furry, familiar, and about my age. Was the robot chasing him? Or was I chasing both of them?

We'd know soon enough. I pounded onward.

The gymnasium loomed ahead.

I closed the distance. Ten feet. Five feet. I reached out.

And I would've caught the cyborg, too. If not for the big fat badger.

Goldie Locket stepped from the gym doorway, arms spread wide.

I was going too fast to stop. So I did the only thing I could—ran straight into her, up her body and onto her head.

"Hold still!" cried the badger. Goldie swatted with her huge paws.

I hopped off her noggin and onto the wall. She cracked herself on the skull.

"Real cute, shamus," she growled.

"That's what I say every time I look in the mirror." I scrambled upward.

Goldie swung, but I was out of reach.

"Where's that kid who was running just now?" I asked.

Her eyes shifted. "What kid?"

"*You're* the one behind the robot?" I said. "Nice trick, using that bad boy to get me bounced out of school. And to think I believed your story about your 'friend' wanting me to cool it."

"But he—" she said. "I mean, uh...took you long enough to figure it out."

Wait a minute. Goldie might be a great goon, but she was a lousy liar.

I pursed my lips. "So tell me, mastermind, how did you make all those kids go loco after lunchtime?"

"I, uh." The badger glowered. "None of your beeswax."

"Uh-huh."

I needed to get inside the gym and catch the real mastermind before he or she scrammed. I needed a distraction.

Looking off down the hall, I said, "Uh-oh. Is that Principal Zero?"

Goldie followed my gaze. Sucker.

In a blink, I zipped down the wall, around the doorframe, and into the gym.

"I don't see—hey!" she cried.

The robot gecko's tail was vanishing out the back door. Dang. I sprinted in pursuit.

Bam! I blew through the door, stumbling out onto the field.

"Got you at last, you—" I stopped cold. "Huh?"

The droid had climbed onto the Yard Czar. And sitting beside it in the driver's seat was the super-average woodchuck, Pete Moss.

He gunned the engine with a wicked grin. "At last we meet, Gecko."

"Pete, we've met before," I said. "Every day in class."

He frowned. "But now you will see what happens when you interfere."

I held up a hand. "Wait, *you*?" I said. "*You're* the evil genius? I'm sorry, but—" I started to laugh.

"It's not funny, Chet! Stop laughing! I am behind it all, and now you will pay."

"Come on," I said, chuckling. "What's with the crazy talk?"

Pete gnashed his teeth. "I asked Goldie to warn you off, but you did not stop investigating. I built this robot to discredit you and split you from your partner. But you still keep sticking your big nose into things."

I felt my schnoz. "My nose isn't that bi—"

"No more!" the woodchuck yelled. "I'll show you. I'll show my aunt. I'll show *everybody*!"

With a grinding roar, the Yard Czar rolled toward me. Gleaming blades and rakes jutted from its sides like a giant, motorized Swiss Army knife.

Pete may have been a joke, but his contraption was deadly serious.

The laughter died in my throat. I turned.

The badger blocked my retreat.

"Goldie," I said, "you can't really be helping this wacko."

She shrugged. "Wacko or no wacko, he pays top dollar. It's hard to find steady work as a thug." Goldie spread her arms and stepped forward.

The machine closed in.

Crouching, I prepared for quick action. Then I heard a sound that froze me in my tracks—literally.

The noon bell rang.

And before its echoes faded, the witches' curse took effect.

My legs and arms went stiffer than a freeze-dried centipede. My body was being squeezed like an old toothpaste tube, longer and longer. I fell to the ground, writhing.

Pete's puzzled mug peered over the Yard Czar's steering wheel, but he kept right on coming.

My legs were useless. I stared up at the grille of the oncoming monster.

Closer and closer it rumbled.

Was this the end of Chet Gecko?

17

The Worminator

Then I got a bright idea. True, I couldn't run, but worms don't run; they crawl.

I twisted my body and humped along on my belly, knees, and chest. Up and down, up and down.

Fweee! The machine's rotating hedge trimmers missed me by a hair. They sliced up a soccer ball and sprayed its bits all over.

I crawled faster.

Pete wheeled his big hunk of junk. Goldie was lumbering toward me.

I made for some krangleberry bushes. I knew I didn't have the chance of a snow cone in a roomful of overheated kindergartners. But I had to try.

Fwap, fwap, fwap! Soft wingbeats reached my ears.

"Hang on, Chet!" a familiar voice called.

Then, *ungh,* something snatched me by my coat and hoisted me into the air.

I looked up. "Natalie!"

She grinned. "The early bird gets the worm."

"But how—?"

Natalie flapped hard. "I got a tip from a little porcupine that two Chet Geckos—*ugh*—went running this way," she panted. "Imagine my—*oomph*—surprise when I saw that one of them was half worm."

"Half?" I said, glancing down at myself.

Natalie was right. I had stumpy arms and legs, and a stretched-out body.

"Too bad you—*oof!*—don't weigh the same as a worm."

Flapping with all her strength, Natalie still couldn't gain much altitude. She struggled upward and sank down again.

"I don't get it," I said. "I'm only *half* worm?"

"Maybe they're—*ugh*—newbie witches. Or maybe it's because you—*oof*—half caught the bad guy."

I glanced back. Goldie was gaining. And Pete and his robot copilot were right behind her.

"Faster, Natalie! To the office!"

She wheeled, heading for the administration building. But she was losing height with every wingbeat. We sank lower, lower.

It was a valiant effort. But we weren't going to make it.

Just then, I spied Ms. DeBree sweeping a walkway.

"Hellllp!" I yelled, as loud as I could. "Ms. De*Bree*!"

The wiry mongoose looked up at us, then at the machine closing in. Her eyes narrowed. "That hamma-jamma contraption!" she cried. "Hang on, kids!"

Pete and Goldie were only a few steps behind us now.

"Hurry!" Natalie gasped.

In one smooth move, the custodian spun her push broom in her paws, cocked it over her shoulder, and took three strides. Then she flung her makeshift spear. "Take *that*!"

The broom soared through the air. For a few heartbeats, I thought it was going to skewer me.

Then it arched lower. *Thunk!*

It plunged straight into the heart of the Yard Czar, skewering its transmission.

Gnitttch-squeeeee! The brute made an awful grinding noise and shuddered to a halt.

Natalie dropped me with a *whump*. She landed, and we turned to watch.

Pete punched the controls. "Go, you stupid rust bucket! Go!"

The Chet robot stared blankly. Goldie started backing away.

Suddenly, Pete Moss, evil genius, looked more like Pete Moss, fourth grader in big trouble.

"Nice shot, Ms. DeBree," I said as she approached.

The custodian shrugged. "Can't beat the old-style technology," she said. "You know what they say . . ."

"There's no tool like an old tool?" Natalie smirked.

Ms. DeBree nodded. "For real." She looked down at me. "Hey, you hit a growth squirt, or what?"

"I'll explain later," I said.

The custodian turned to Pete and Goldie. "You kids, come with me. Principal Zero is gonna want a word or three with you."

She slung the robot over her shoulder, confiscated its controls, and marched the two troublemakers off.

Natalie and I watched them go.

"Thanks, partner," I said. "You really saved my hide."

"Again," she said.

"Again," I agreed. "Well, I guess we should go hunt up the witches."

Natalie looked down at me. "What for?"

"So I can apologize and get them to reverse the curse. Let's motor." I tried to stand, but was still too wormish. "Uh, mind giving me another lift?"

Natalie eyed me the way I eyeball my mom's wolf spider pizza. "What's your hurry?"

"Ha, ha," I said. "Don't kid around."

"But I *like* worms," said Natalie, eyes twinkling. "And you know, I haven't had lunch yet..."

"Natalie...," I said, warningly.

18

That's What Ends Are For

By late recess, I had my own body back, and all was right with the world. Natalie and I kicked a soccer ball around while Maureen DeBree gave us the latest scoop.

"So this whole thing started because Dr. Lightov stole some inventions from Pete's dad?" said Natalie.

Ms. DeBree stabbed a gum wrapper with her trash pole and twitched it into her bag. "That's what it sounded like through the kid's blubbering," she said. "The bugger wanted revenge—plus he wanted to be noticed, in the worst way."

"Let's see," said Natalie. "He sabotaged the inventions, put chemicals in the Munchmeister meals to make kids act rowdy, and tried to grind us up in the Yard Czar. I'd say that's the worst way."

I hooked the ball with my foot and bounced it off my knee, happy to have knees again.

"But how did Pete come up with the formula that made everyone go nuts?" I said.

"And the robot?" said Natalie. "That couldn't have been easy to make."

I kicked the ball to her. "Yeah, after all, Pete isn't exactly a whiz kid."

The custodian bent to scrape gum off the walk-way. "Chee, the little stinkers," she muttered.

"Ms. DeBree?" I said.

She looked up. "Eh? Oh, yeah. Turns out the bugger really *is* one genius. He never tries in class, 'cause it's too easy for him."

"Huh," I said. "Looks can be deceiving."

Natalie chirped, "I'll say. Look at *you*." She passed the ball back.

"Funny, birdie."

We kicked it around some more while Ms. De-Bree tidied up the bushes.

"So what happens to the money-saving inventions?" said Natalie.

The mongoose lifted a shoulder. "That gal, Dr. Lightov, she got in bad disrefute from this whole thing."

"You mean, the woodchuck's in the doghouse?" I said.

"That's what I'm saying," said Ms. DeBree.

"They're gonna hire back everyone who was fired and trash all the fancy new machines."

"Even the robot?" I said. "I could think of a few uses for him..."

"*Especially* the robot," said the mongoose. "Mr. Zero said one Chet Gecko at this school is plenty."

Dang. Ah, well. Can't blame a PI for trying.

"So I guess we go back to doing things the old-fashioned way," said Natalie.

"With animal power," Ms. DeBree said, tying up her trash bag.

I looked from my partner to our custodian—mockingbird and mongoose, true-blue friends, both of them.

"Animal power works for me," I said with a smile.

Look for more mysteries from
the Tattered Casebook of Chet Gecko
in hardcover and paperback

Case #1   *The Chameleon Wore Chartreuse*

Some cases start rough, some cases start easy. This one started with a dame. (That's what we private eyes call a girl.) She was cute and green and scaly. She looked like trouble and smelled like . . . grasshoppers.

Shirley Chameleon came to me when her little brother, Billy, turned up missing. She turned on the tears. She promised me some stinkbug pie. I said I'd find the brat.

But when his trail led to a certain stinky-breathed, bad-tempered, jumbo-sized Gila monster, I thought I'd bitten off more than I could chew. Worse, I had to chew fast: If I didn't find Billy in time, it would be bye-bye, stinkbug pie.

Case #2   *The Mystery of Mr. Nice*

How would you know if some criminal mastermind tried to impersonate your principal? My first clue: He was nice to me.

This fiend tried everything—flattery, friendship, food—but he still couldn't keep me off the case. Natalie and I followed a trail of clues as thin as the cheese on a cafeteria hamburger. And we found a ring of corruption that went from the janitor right up to Mr. Big.

In the nick of time, we rescued Principal Zero and busted up the PTA meeting, putting a stop to the evil genius. And what thanks did we get? Just the usual. A cold handshake and a warm soda.

But that's all in a day's work for a private eye.

Case #3   *Farewell, My Lunchbag*

If danger is my business, then dinner is my passion. I'll take any case if the pay is right. And what pay could be better than Mothloaf Surprise?

At least that's what I thought. But in this particular case, I almost paid the ultimate price for good grub.

Cafeteria lady Mrs. Bagoong hired me to track down whoever was stealing her food supplies. The long, slimy trail led too close to my own backyard for comfort.

And much, much too close to Jimmy "King" Cobra. Without the help of Natalie Attired and our school janitor, Maureen DeBree, I would've been gecko sushi.

Case #4   *The Big Nap*

My grades were lower than a salamander's slippers, and my bank account was trying to crawl under a duck's belly. So why did I take a case that didn't pay anything?

Put it this way: Would *you* stand by and watch some evil power turn *your* classmates into hypnotized zombies? (If that wasn't just what normally happened to them in math class, I mean.)

My investigations revealed a plot meaner than a roomful of rhinos with diaper rash.

Someone at Emerson Hicky was using a sinister video game to put more and more students into la-la-land. And it was up to me to stop it, pronto—before that someone caught up with me, and I found myself taking the Big Nap.

Case #5 *The Hamster of the Baskervilles*

Elementary school is a wild place. But this was ridiculous.

Someone—or some*thing*—was tearing up Emerson Hicky. Classrooms were trashed. Walls were gnawed. Mysterious tunnels riddled the playground like worm chunks in a pan of earthworm lasagna.

But nobody could spot the culprit, let alone catch him.

Then, a teacher reported seeing a monster on full-moon night, and I got the call.

At the end of a twisted trail of clues, I had to answer the burning question: Was it a vicious, supernatural were-hamster on the loose, or just another Science Fair project gone wrong?

Case #6 *This Gum for Hire*

Never thought I'd see the day when one of my worst enemies would hire me for a case. Herman the Gila

Monster was a sixth-grade hoodlum with a first-rate left hook. He told me someone was disappearing the football team, and he had to put a stop to it. *Big whoop.*

He told me he was being blamed for the kidnappings, and he had to clear his name. *Boo hoo.*

Then he said that I could either take the case and earn a nice reward, or have my face rearranged like a bargain-basement Picasso painted by a spastic chimp.

I took the case.

But before I could find the kidnapper, I had to go undercover. And that meant facing something that scared me worse than a chorus line of criminals in steel-toed boots: P.E. class.

Case #7   *The Malted Falcon*

It was tall, dark, and chocolatey—the stuff dreams are made of. It was a treat so titanic that nobody had been able to finish one single-handedly (or even single-mouthedly). It was the Malted Falcon.

How far would you go for the ultimate dessert? Somebody went too far, and that's where I came in.

The local sweets shop held a contest. The prize: a year's supply of free Malted Falcons. Some lucky kid scored the winning ticket. She brought it to school for show-and-tell.

But after she showed it, somebody swiped it.

Following a strong hunch and an even stronger sweet tooth, I tracked the ticket through a web of lies more tangled than a rattlesnake doing the rumba. But the time to claim the prize was fast approaching. Would the villain get the sweet treat—or his just desserts?

Case #8 *Trouble Is My Beeswax*

Okay, I confess. When test time rolls around, I'm as tempted as the next lizard to let my eyeballs do the walking . . . to my neighbor's paper.

But Mrs. Gecko didn't raise no cheaters. (Some language manglers, perhaps.) So when a routine investigation uncovered a test-cheating ring at Emerson Hicky, I gave myself a new case: Put the cheaters out of business.

Easier said than done. Those double-dealers were slicker than a frog's fanny and twice as slimy.

Oh, and there was one other small problem: All the evidence pointed to two dames. The ringleader was either the glamorous Lacey Vail, or my own classmate Shirley Chameleon.

Sheesh. The only thing I hate worse than an empty Pillbug Crunch wrapper is a case full of dizzy dames.

Case #9 *Give My Regrets to Broadway*

Some things you can't escape, however hard you try—like dentist appointments, visits with strange-smelling relatives, and being in the fourth-grade play. I had always left the acting to my smart-aleck pal, Natalie, but now it was my turn in the spotlight.

Stage fright? Me? You're talking about a gecko

who has laughed at danger, chuckled at catastrophe, and sneezed at sinister plots.

I was terrified.

Not because of the acting, mind you. The script called for me to share a major lip-lock with Shirley Chameleon—Cootie Queen of the Universe!

And while I was trying to avoid that trap, a simple missing persons case took a turn for the worse—right into the middle of my play. Would opening night spell curtains for my client? No matter what happens, the sleuth must go on.

Case #10 *Murder, My Tweet*

Some things at school you can count on. Pop quizzes always pop up just after you've spent your study time studying comics. Chef's Surprise is always a surprise, but never a good one. And no matter how much you learn today, they always make you come back tomorrow.

But sometimes, Emerson Hicky amazes you. And just like finding a killer bee in a box of Earwig Puffs, you're left shocked, stung, and discombobulated.

Foul play struck at my school; that's nothing new. But then the finger of suspicion pointed straight at my favorite fowl: Natalie Attired. Framed as a blackmailer, my partner was booted out of Emerson Hicky quicker than a hoptoad on a hot plate.

I tackled the case for free. Mess with my partner, mess with me.

Then things took a turn for the worse. Just when I thought I might clear her name, Natalie disappeared. And worse still, she left behind one clue: a reddish smear that looked kinda like the jelly from a beetle-jelly sandwich but raised an ugly question: Was it murder, or something serious?

Case #11 *The Possum Always Rings Twice*

In my time, I've tackled cases stickier than a spider's handshake and harder than three-year-old boll weevil taffy. But nothing compares to the job that landed me knee-deep in school politics.

What seemed like a straightforward case of extortion during Emerson Hicky's student-council election ended up taking more twists and turns than an anaconda's lunch. It became a battle royal for control of the school. (Not that I necessarily believe school is worth fighting for, but a gecko's gotta do *something* with his days.)

Was I savvy enough to escape with my skin? Let me put it this way: Just like a politician, this is one private eye who always shoots from the lip.

Case #12 *Key Lardo*

Working this case, I nearly lost my detective mojo— and to a guy so dim, he'd probably play goalie for the darts team. True, he was only a cog in a larger conspiracy. But this big buttinsky made my life more uncomfortable than a porcupine's underpants.

Was he a cop? A truant officer? A gorilla with a grudge? Even worse: A rival detective. His name was Bland. *James* Bland. And he was cracking cases faster than a . . . well, *much* faster than I was.

My reputation took a nosedive. And I nearly followed it—straight into the slammer. Fighting back with all my moxie, I bent the rules, blundered into blind alleys, and stepped on more than a few toes.

Was I right? Was I wrong? I'll tell you this: I made my share of mistakes. But I believe that if you can't laugh at yourself . . . make fun of someone else.

Case #13   *Hiss Me Deadly*

When my sister got robbed, she turned to me for help. And like a dope, I jumped in with both feet.

But a simple case of theft soon grew more challenging than playing Chinese Checkers on a bucking bronco. Valuables started vanishing from school, and the top brass called me in. I followed the twisty trail of clues until I'd unearthed more suspects than a zombie membership drive.

The heat was on. As I drew closer to uncovering the shadowy puppet master behind it all, I got myself in a spot tighter than a blue whale's bikini.

Not to worry. As any detective will tell you, it's always darkest before dawn. So if you're going to steal your neighbor's newspaper, that's the time to do it.